LITTLE TIGER PRESS • An imprint of Magi Publications
1 The Coda Centre, 189 Munster Road, London SW6 6AW
www.littletigerpress.com
First published in Great Britain 2009 • This edition published 2009
Text copyright © Paul Bright 2009 • Illustrations copyright © Lee Wildish 2009
Paul Bright and Lee Wildish have asserted their rights to be identified
as the author and illustrator of this work under the Copyright,
Designs and Patents Act, 1988 • A CIP catalogue record for this
book is available from the British Library • All rights reserved
ISBN 978-1-84506-980-3
Printed in China
2 4 6 8 10 9 7 5 3 1

For Katie, with love ~ P B

For Laura, Grace and Oscar ~ L W

CHARLIE'S SUPERHERO UNDERPANTS

Paul Bright

Lee Wildish

LITTLE TIGER PRESS

London

On a wild and windy day,
round about the end of May,
A great and gusting gale
blew the washing clean away.

Socks and vests, a woolly hat,
but far worse than all of that,
Young Charlie's Superhero Underpants.

POW!

As it soared into the sky,
the washing billowed, flapped and swirled,
Until it slowly scattered
to the corners of the world.

Though they searched for days and nights, and planes and satellites, with boats

They found **no trace** of Charlie's Underpants.

They had **POW!**
across the front,
in giant letters,
bold and black,

With KERZAP! and OOF!
and SPLAT! a little smaller
on the back.

And villains would take fright
as Charlie pulled his pants up tight.
His Scarlet Superhero
Underpants.

Charlie packed
some sandwiches,
some sardines
and some soap,

A mirror, fan and toothbrush,
and a big brass telescope.

"Don't worry and don't wait," he said,
"I may be back quite late.
But I've got to find my
Scarlet Underpants."

First Charlie grabbed a ride
with a band in a balloon,
And they crossed the choppy Channel
to a bouncy, brassy tune.

There they spied
a fine French fox,
wearing sister Sophie's socks,
But they saw no sign of Charlie's Underpants.

Angleterre

Culotte

Charlie hiked across
the endless plain of Serengeti,
Where the insects made him itchy
and the sunshine made him sweaty.

And there he saw a lion,
with a stripy shirt and tie on,
But no Scarlet Superhero Underpants.

Charlie climbed and clambered
up the plateau of Peru,
Where the breeze that blows at night
makes you shiver through and through,

And an alligator sat,
wearing Grandpa's woolly hat,
But it wasn't wearing Charlie's Underpants.

Charlie was fed up.
He felt lonely, tired and small,
On a steep and snowy hillside
in the mountains of Nepal.

When suddenly he saw,
in that land of ice and cold,
A huge and hairy creature,
something wondrous to behold.

Charlie blinked and rubbed his eyes.
It couldn't be . . .

it could . . .

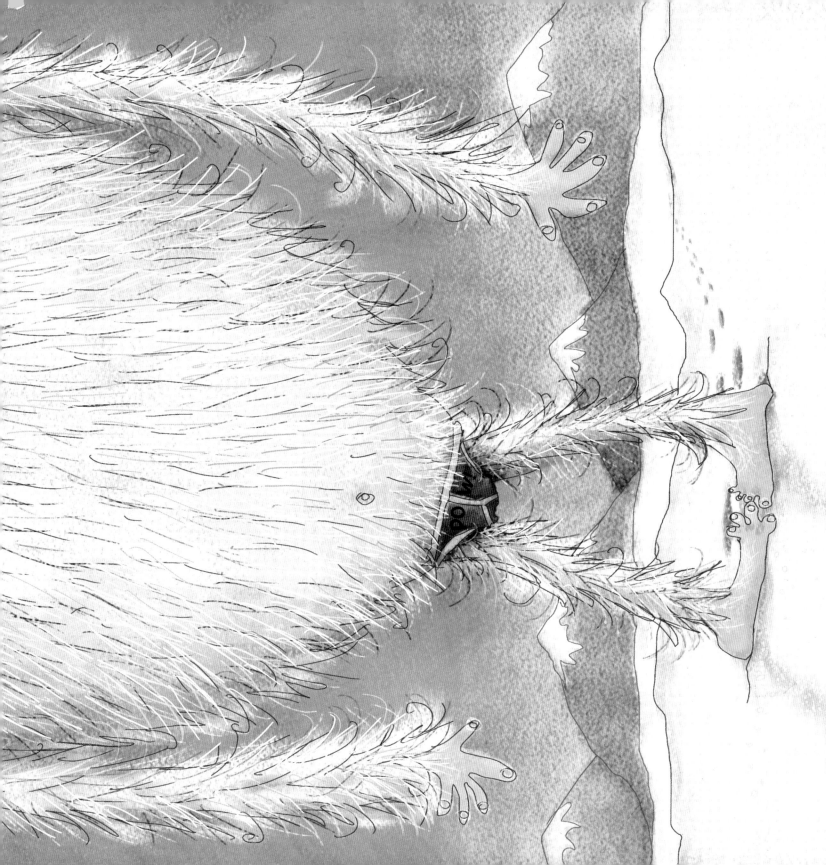

For there, in Charlie's Underpants, a Yeti proudly stood.

"My underpants!" cried Charlie.
"They're the ones I love the most."

"But they're mine now," growled the Yeti, "and they keep me warm as toast!"

"I'll swap you," Charlie said.
"You'll be snug from toes to head,
If you'll give me back my Scarlet Underpants."

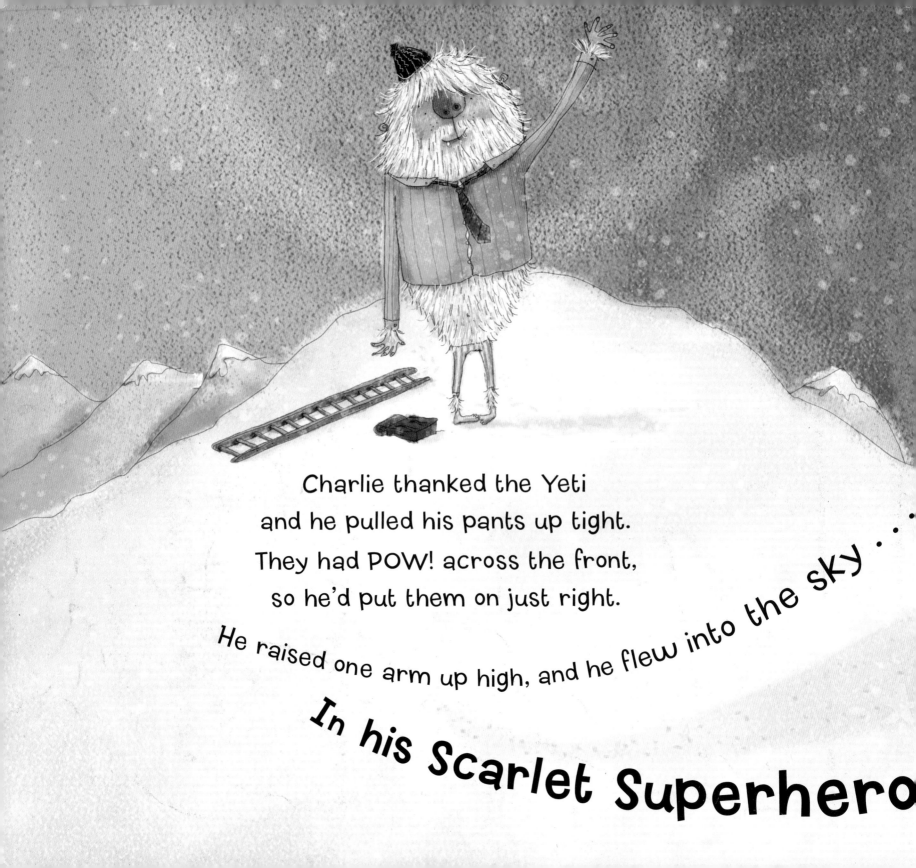

Charlie thanked the Yeti
and he pulled his pants up tight.
They had POW! across the front,
so he'd put them on just right.

He raised one arm up high, and he flew into the sky . . .

In his Scarlet Superhero

And he found
a pair of llamas
wearing brother Ben's pyjamas,

But he couldn't find his
Scarlet Underpants.

Charlie searched the length
of the mighty Mississippi,
Though the Mississippi's muddy
and the mud's all soft and slippy,

Underpants!

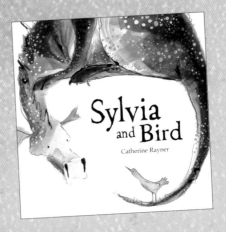

Sylvia and Bird

Catherine Rayner

The Three Horrid Pigs
and the Big Friendly Wolf

by Liz Pichon

The Bears in the Bed and the Great BIG Storm

Paul Bright
Jane Chapman

Take a look at these SUPER books from Little Tiger Press!

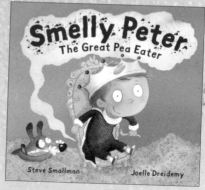

Smelly Peter
The Great Pea Eater

Steve Smallman   Joelle Dreidemy

Simon Prescott

Small Mouse
BIG CITY

Paul Bright
Mike Terry

CRUNCH MUNCH
DINOSAUR LUNCH!

For information regarding any
of the above titles or for our
catalogue, please contact us:
Little Tiger Press, 1 The Coda Centre,
189 Munster Road, London SW6 6AW
Tel: 020 7385 6333 Fax: 020 7385 7333
E-mail: info@littletiger.co.uk
www.littletigerpress.com